THE MYSTERIOUS TALENT SHOW MYSTERY

by Tony Abbott

illustrated by Colleen Madden

EGMONT
New York USA

To all my goofily talented friends at Egmont!—T.A.

EGMONT
We bring stories to life
First published by Egmont USA, 2013
443 Park Avenue South, Suite 806
New York, NY 10016

1 3 5 7 9 8 6 4 2

www.egmontusa.com
www.goofballsbytonyabbott.blogspot.com
www.greenfrographics.com

Library of Congress Cataloging-in-Publication Data
Abbott, Tony
The mysterious talent show mystery / Tony Abbott;
illustrated by Colleen Madden.
p. cm. -- (Goofballs ; bk. 4)
Summary: The Goofballs are lucky they are expert detectives when their school talent show becomes a whirlwind of mysterious events!
ISBN 978-1-60684-167-9 (hardback) -- ISBN 978-1-60684-400-7 (digest paperback) -- ISBN 978-1-60684-401-4 (electronic book)
[1. Mystery and detective stories. 2. Talent shows--Fiction. 3. Schools--Fiction. 4. Humorous stories.] I. Madden, Colleen M., ill. II. Title.
PZ7.A1587Mys 2013
[Fic]--dc23
2012024560

Printed in the United States of America

Book design by Alison Chamberlain

Contents

1

Something Goofy

Hi, I'm Jeff Bunter.

And you're not.

That's a goofy joke.

But it's no joke that I'm an official Goofball.

My friends Brian Rooney, Kelly Smitts, and Mara Lubin are also official Goofballs.

We solve mysteries like nobody else.

Brian is an inventor. Sort of.

He makes wacky junk that doesn't always work but looks really cool and helps us solve crimes.

Kelly is as smart as a computer, but she doesn't look like one. Unless a computer is really short, really suspicious, and has big yellow hair. Which sounds like an invention Brian would make.

Then there's Mara. She's tall like a fashion model, as skinny as a rake handle, and wears giant green glasses. She's also a master of amazing disguises.

Me, I was born to solve mysteries.

Since I first learned to carry stuff, I've carried a notebook around with me. I call it my cluebook because I write down all the clues I find. And believe me, there are clues everywhere!

Like the ones we found last week.

It was the first rehearsal for the Badger Point Elementary School Talent Show.

We couldn't have the show at our own school because they were putting down a new floor in the Cafeteri-Audi-Nasium.

"Good thing," Brian said when he found out. "Without a floor, we'd fall into the basement."

So, instead of being held at Badger Point Elementary, our show would be at the big, large, huge, and enormous Badger Point High School!

That's where Brian, Kelly, Mara, and I met last Monday afternoon for our first rehearsal.

In my backpack were a dinner plate and a balancing stick. I was really getting good at spinning that plate. I wanted everyone to see me do it.

Of course, being Goofballs, we all agreed to keep our talents secret, even from one another. It was more mysterious that way.

But none of us guessed what the *real* talent show mystery would be.

"Someday, we'll go to this school," said Kelly as we looked up at the big building.

"*Sun*day?" said Brian. "That's a week from now. I can't wait that long."

And he walked right in, leaving the doors swinging behind him.

"Brian's a Goofball," said Mara.

"Also a glueball," I said. "Which means we should probably stick together."

The moment we entered the high school, Kelly gasped. "Wows!"

Wows, is right.

The school was humongous. Inside the front doors were three super-long hallways leading off into the distance.

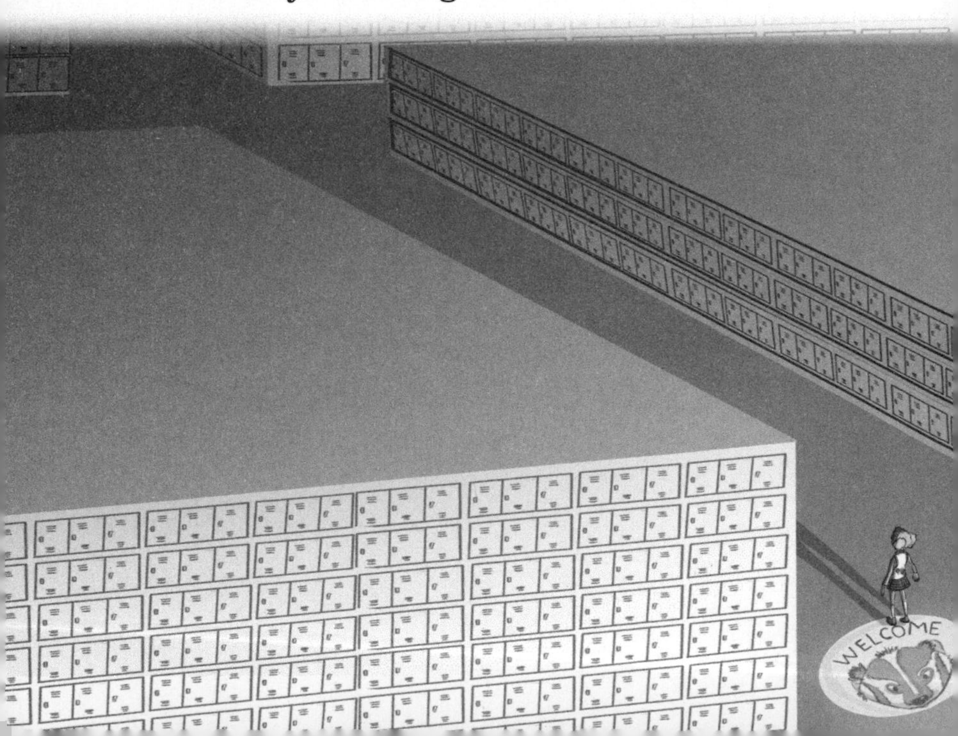

Brian stared down each hall. "Does anyone know where the auditorium is?" he asked.

"I was here once," I said. "So I do."

"I do, too," Mara said.

"Me, too," Kelly said.

"Well, I don't," said Brian. "So I should lead the way." He started down the wrong hall.

"Brian, wait," I said. "If you're the only one who *doesn't* know where the auditorium is, why should *you* lead?"

Brian smiled at me. "Jeff, Jeff. It's simple."

Uh-oh. When Brian says, "It's simple," it's usually the opposite.

"First of all," he said, "where are we at this exact moment?"

"In the high school," said Mara.

"And what are schools for?" said Brian.

"To learn things," said Kelly.

"But since you already *know* where the auditorium is, you can't *learn* where it is," Brian said. "Since I *don't* know where it is, I'll *learn* where it is. That's why I should lead."

I stared at Brian.

Kelly stared at Brian.

Mara stared at Brian.

"I'm glad we're all agreed," Brian said. Then he took a pair of cardboard binoculars from his cargo pants, pretended to focus them, and crept down the completely wrong hall like he was tracking a jungle beast.

Kelly sighed. “If we don’t follow him, he’ll get lost.”

Mara sighed, too. “If we *do* follow him, *we’ll* get lost.”

I sighed the loudest. “I know I’m going to sound like Brian here, but the Goofballs are nowhere unless we’re all together, so it’s better to find ourselves lost together with Brian than to lose Brian and find ourselves together without him.”

Kelly stared at me.

Mara stared at me.

"Plus *maybe* we won't get lost," I said.

So we followed Brian.

And we got lost.

We started by going upstairs to the second floor. There we discovered a hall with no lights and no doors. Then we found a hall with lots of doors but no lights. Then we found a hall with no doors but lots of lights. Then we found the stairway back to the front doors again and went right to the auditorium.

"This is like a corn maze," Brian said.

"*Maize* is the Indian word for corn," Kelly said.

"*Corny* is my word for goofy," I said.

"And *mystery* is my word for that!" said Mara. She pointed to a sign outside the auditorium doors.

"Friturday?" Mara stared at the sign through her big green glasses. "And I thought *I* had talent. Someone is inventing new days!"

"Maybe it's our first clue," whispered Kelly.

At the word *clue*, I pulled out my cluebook and scribbled it down.

Friturday Night
Our first clue?

"It might just be a spelling mistake," I said.

"I sometimes misspell my name," said Brian. "And *Brian* comes out *Brain*. But it's not really a mistake. Because I really *am* a brain!"

No one said anything for a few seconds.

"Maybe," Kelly grumbled finally. "But mistake or not, I've got my eyes on that sign."

"I've got my eyes on my face," said Brian. "They're easier to blink that way. Watch . . ."

He blinked over and over and over.

It made us all a little sick, but we couldn't look away.

Brian finally got so dizzy with blinking that he fell over. We helped him to his feet.

"Come on, *Brain*," I said. "You can hurt your *Brian* that way."

"Me, too," he said as we all entered the auditorium.

2

The Mystery of the Missing Talent

The auditorium was as huge as a football field. Except that it was indoors and had rows of seats from wall to wall and a stage big enough to land a plane on.

Our classmates Billy Carlson, Joey Myers, and Tiffany Flynn were already there.

Tiffany wore tap shoes that clacked whenever she took a step.

Billy held a piece of rope. And Joey kept moving his lips and laughing to himself.

Billy and Joey had figured in a couple of our mysteries before. They weren't all that goofy, but they were okay anyway. Tiffany was pretty new in our class, so I hadn't noticed if she was goofy or not.

Finally, Violet Boggs walked onstage.

Even though her name was Violet, she always wore pink from head to toe.

"I'm going to the opening of Pinkworld next week," she said. "It's a store that sells all kinds of pink stuff."

Kelly looked her up and down. "Is there any left?"

"Some," said Violet. "I'm getting it."

Then Violet dragged a big lumpy thing to the center of the stage.

It looked like a baby elephant on wheels.

"Is that a baby elephant on wheels?" I asked.

"It's my pink tuba," said Violet. She lifted away a fuzzy pink blanket, opened the case, and removed what looked like a pink smokestack attached to a pink radiator attached to pink bathroom plumbing.

"Cool invention," said Brian. "What does it sound like?"

"Just listen!" Violet twisted herself into the tuba and puffed into the mouthpiece.

BWAAAP!

Brian fell over again. "Oww," he said, rubbing his head. "I really need to rest my Brian."

"Plus it hurts my mind," said Tiffany, slapping her hands over her ears.

The curtain whooshed aside, and our principal, Principal Higgins, appeared on the stage. "Hello, children. I want to introduce Tabitha Rinkle, the director of the talent show—"

All at once, a short, round lady with big red hair flew past the principal and bounced across the stage to us.

"I am Mrs. Tabitha Rinkle, the director of the talent show!" she said with a big laugh. "Come to me!"

We did. But Principal Higgins didn't. He said he had principal stuff to do, and he left the auditorium.

"As you know," Mrs. Rinkle said, changing her laugh to a smile, "this is an awesome theater. It has a backstage, a fog machine, a music room, and a costume shop, and even a catwalk!"

"I don't have a cat," said Kelly. "But if I did, could I walk it here?"

Mrs. Tabitha Rinkle laughed again. "No, no, dear! A catwalk is a walkway for the stage crew. It's high above the stage. See?"

We looked up. The catwalk was a skinny bridge way up behind the main curtain.

"Now, there will be two acts in our show," Mrs. Rinkle said.

"That's a lot," said Billy Carlson.

"Act one is the talent show," Mrs. Rinkle continued. "Act two is a play. Let's start with act one talent auditions. Tiffany Flynn?"

We all stood aside as Tiffany clacked to the center of the stage and clicked on a CD player.

First music started.

Then Tiffany started.

To dance.

Sort of.

Her right foot tapped like crazy.

Tappa-tappa-tap-te-tappa-tap!

Her arms flew all around like wings. But her left foot didn't move an inch.

It sat like a lump of stone glued to the stage.

"One of her feet doesn't seem to be working," Mara whispered.

Tappa-tappity-ta-tappppp!

Tiffany bowed suddenly, and her dance was over.

"Awesome! Awesome! Awesome!" Mrs. Rinkle said, using what we would soon learn was her favorite word. "Next is Billy Carlson."

Billy bowed. "I call my act 'Taming the Wild Snake.'"

He swished his rope back and forth on the floor in front of him. "Oh, no. A wild snake. Watch while I tame it."

Billy pulled the rope up. It hung limply in his hands. "Thank you."

"Write this down, Jeff," whispered Kelly.

Tiffany — one-foot tap dance
Billy — rope trick?

"I shall now tell a series of jokes," Joey Myers said with a bow. "Here I go. Why did the farmer drive a red truck with a green steering wheel?"

"Why?" we asked.

"Because it was a long way to town. Why is the sky blue?"

"Why?" we asked.

"Because all the other colors were taken. Why do restaurants serve food?"

"Why?" we asked.

"Because barber shops are too busy. Why did the elephant sit down?"

“Why?” we asked.

“Because it was a long way to town. Why were the twins named Henri with an *i* and Henry with a *y*?”

“Why?” we asked.

“So their mother could tell them apart. Thank you.”

When Joey walked off, Violet carried her big pink tuba to the center of the stage and slid herself into it.

"In the hands of a master," she said, "the tuba can meow like a tiny kitten. . . ."

BWAAAAP!

"It can play a military march. . . ."

BWAAAAP!

"It can also play a soft lullaby. . . ."

BWAAAAP!

I wondered if Mrs. Rinkle would ask the Goofballs to search for all the missing talent. But she just laughed and said, "Awesome!"

Then it was our turn.

"I'll be singing a song," Kelly said.

"What is it called?" asked Mrs. Rinkle.

"It doesn't matter," said Kelly.

"I've never heard that song before," Mrs. Rinkle said.

That's because *no one* had heard that song before.

Not even Kelly.

Because she made it up as she sang it.

I'm on a big stage . . .
There are seats out there . . .
My neck kind of itches . . .
I have blond hair . . .

"Lovely rhyme. Thank you, dear," said Mrs. Rinkle.

"But there's a second verse!" said Kelly.

It's way after school . . .
I like watermelon . . .
Polar bears are white . . .
My name's not Ellen . . .

We all clapped before Kelly could sing the third verse.

"Now . . . Brian," said Mrs. Rinkle.

All at once, I heard something snap. I spun around to see Brian with the balancing stick from my backpack. He had snapped it in half and was snapping the pieces in half again.

"What are you doing?" I screamed.

"I need a couple of very short sticks," he said, breaking the pieces in half one more time. Now they were tiny slivers.

"But that's half my act!" I cried.

"Don't worry, Jeff," he said. "My act will completely knock their socks off. While everyone runs home for new socks, we'll find another stick for you."

I was about to explode, but Brian dashed onstage. He held up the tiny sticks and tapped them together.

Then his hands began to swordfight!

Brian pretended his hands were two guys in a duel. He even did the voices of each hand out of different sides of his mouth. "Take *zat*!"

"No, *you* take *zis*!"

"I'll *vin* zis duel!"

"No, *I* vill vin!"

It was like . . . it was like . . . I don't know what it was like.

Finally, both hands lowered their swords. Brian said, "Thank you."

So did his hands.

"*Tank* you!"

"*Sank* you!"

"Thrilling!" said Mrs. Rinkle.

Mara was next. "I will model this scarf," she said, lightly touching a green scarf wound around her neck.

She stood there. And stood there some more. And kept on standing.

"Thank you," she said, and she walked off the stage.

Mrs. Rinkle clapped for a full minute. "Very elegant, my dear! Just brilliant! Now . . . Jeff?"

I glared at Brian. "No one's socks came off," I said.

Brian shrugged. "Probably a good thing."

But Goofballs don't stay mad at other Goofballs. And they never give up, no matter how much Brian wrecks stuff.

"My act is . . . *not* . . . spinning a plate," I said. I set the plastic plate on the stage. It just sat there. "Look how *not* spinning it is!"

After a minute, I bowed and left the stage.

But Mrs. Rinkle jumped from her seat, shouting, "Excellent! Wonderful! And, well, awesome! I can't wait to share you with the audience next Friday night!" she said.

Joey turned to Mrs. Rinkle. "You mean Saturday night, right? It sort of says that on the sign."

Mrs. Rinkle held up the sign we saw outside. "I'm sorry. I thought the show was *both* Friday and Saturday nights. So I started to spell them both. Then I found out that the high school needs the theater next Saturday night. So our show will be only on Friday."

She changed the spelling on the sign.

But little did we know that when Mrs. Tabitha Rinkle took the "tur" out of *Friturday*, the Mysterious Talent Show Mystery was about to begin!

3

Things Start to Happen

When we arrived on Tuesday afternoon, we found Mrs. Rinkle stamping her foot over and over on the stage.

"Are you trying to learn Tiffany's dance?" asked Mara.

"Or stomping Billy's wild snake?" asked Kelly.

Mrs. Rinkle laughed. "Neither. My foot fell asleep!"

"That's because it's dark inside your shoe, and your foot thought it was bedtime," said Brian.

"That's it!" Mrs. Rinkle said. "Now, gather around. Today we'll rehearse the act two play. It's called *Mr. Bat's Birthday Rescue*. Each of you has a role based on his or her talent. Violet, would you please pass out the scripts so everyone can see his or her part?"

"Yes, ma'am," Violet said, and she passed out the scripts so we could read our names.

```
Tiffany  —  Miss Zebra
Kelly    —  Miss River Fairy
Violet   —  Miss Giraffe
Brian    —  Mr. Bat
```

Billy	—	Mr. Monkey
Joey	—	Mr. Wood Elf
Mara	—	Miss Tree
Jeff	—	Mr. Panda

"Now, let's get measured for costumes," Mrs. Rinkle said as she led us all into the costume room. "Tiffany has agreed to make all your animal suits for the show," she said.

Tiffany beamed. "I have my own sewing machine and everything."

She passed around a tape measure and took down the measurements on a piece of yellow paper on a clipboard.

We measured our arms and legs.

We measured our hands and feet.

We measured our waists and heads.

"I win!" said Brian. "My head is the biggest."

"I could have told you that," I said.

"Unless you count my hair," said Kelly, fluffing her big curls.

"That would take too long," said Mara. "Did you know the human head contains an average of 120,000 hairs?"

"Maybe that's true," said Kelly, "but there's nothing average about Goofballs, so I probably have more."

When we finished measuring, Mrs. Rinkle said, "Tiffany, can you sew all the costumes by the end of the week?"

"Of course I can," Tiffany said.

"Good," Mrs. Rinkle said. "We'll try on our costumes this Friday and have our dress rehearsal next Thursday."

"*Dress* rehearsal?" said Brian. "Boys don't wear dresses. Is there a pants rehearsal, too?"

Mrs. Rinkle shook with laughter as she led us back to the stage. "A dress rehearsal is what we call our first rehearsal when we dress up in our costumes. Now let's read our play!"

But the instant we opened our scripts, Billy started to blink, then groan, then wobble.

"I can't go on!" he said.

"The show *always* goes on," said Mrs. Rinkle. "Billy, what's the matter?"

"I'm Mr. Monkey, and Mr. Monkey has too many words!" Billy said. "Listen to them all."

```
Dear Mr. Bat. Do not be afraid.
All your friends have come to
rescue you. I will climb the
tree. Then I will tame the
wild snake so you won't be
scared. Then we'll climb down
the tree together. We will have
coconut pancakes by the river.
All your best friends will be
there. Are you ready? Here I
come.
```

Joey frowned. "What a great part," he said.

"It's too many words all at once," Billy said.

"You don't say them all at once," said Kelly. "You say them one at a time."

Mrs. Rinkle patted Billy's shoulder. "We'll be rehearsing for nearly two weeks. You'll have plenty of time to learn your part."

"Maybe," said Billy. He started wobbling again, but Joey kept him from falling.

Mrs. Rinkle took a deep breath. "Now, who would like to read the beginning of our play?"

"I would," said Mara.

And she read aloud from her script.

"'*Mr. Bat's Birthday Rescue*. Scene one. A jungle at dawn. The air is filled with the gentle calls of birds waking up.'"

"That's a cue for Violet," said Mrs. Rinkle.

Brian laughed. "A *Q* for Violet? Shouldn't it be a *V* for Violet?"

"No, *Brain*," said Kelly. "A *cue* is a signal for an actor to begin a speech."

"Or in this case," said Mrs. Rinkle, "a signal to begin our jungle music—the gentle birdcalls that open the play. Violet? Your tuba?"

That's when a *cue* turned into a *clue*!

Because instead of *bwaap*ing her pink tuba, Violet screamed at the top of her lungs.

"My tuba is gone! Someone took it! Someone hid it! The show can't possibly go on!"

We all ran into the music room and stared at the empty tuba case.

I wrote it down instantly.

Pink tuba gone
Also fuzzy pink blanket

"But Violet, dear, are you sure you didn't just misplace it?" asked Mrs. Rinkle.

Violet blinked. "How do you misplace a gigantic pink tuba? It's bigger than me!"

Tiffany took the tape measure from around her neck and measured first the tuba case, then Violet. "She's right. It *is* bigger than her!"

Then I remembered how Tiffany said the tuba playing hurt her mind.

Was that a clue?

Mara nodded firmly. "As an official Goofball, I say we need to search for Violet's tuba."

"I'll help the search," Billy said to us. "I'll search the theater office."

“I’ll search backstage, high and low,” said Joey.

“I’ll search every inch of the costume room,” said Tiffany.

“I’ll come with the Goofballs,” said Violet.

“Because you know the Goofballs will find your tuba?” I asked.

“Uh . . . sure,” said Violet. “Follow me!”

Violet dashed out of the auditorium and down the hall.

We had to rush to keep up with her.

“This is *not* the way we search for clues! Or tubas!” Mara said. “It’s *highly* not normal!”

But Violet rushed down the halls, first one way, then another.

We ran after her. We went through classrooms and into gyms and cafeterias and kitchens and closets.

I wrote down everything we found.

Nothing
Nothing
And nothing

"Violet, when did you first see that the tuba was gone?" Kelly asked.

"When my eyes told me it wasn't there," said Violet.

"Your eyes tell you stuff?" said Brian. "Now, *that's* a talent."

Violet grabbed the handle of a narrow black door and snorted. "Locked. Keep searching."

Like Brian, Violet would get an A+ for what she learned. She zigzagged all over the school until she learned every inch of it.

We didn't find her pink tuba.

But we *did* discover something else.

When we finally made it back to the auditorium, I tried to open the door to get back in. But I couldn't. The door was locked.

Kelly knocked on the door, and Billy answered it, a pile of copy paper in his hands. "Did you have any luck?"

"The Goofballs don't need luck," Mara said. "We are detective experts."

"Oh," said Billy. "Did you have any luck being detective experts?"

We all shook our heads.

"This is a disaster!" said Violet, storming onto the stage. "We have to delay the show. I can't play my tuba without my tuba!"

While Violet talked with Mrs. Rinkle, I turned to the Goofballs.

"Something is bothering me," I said.

"We'll find another balancing stick," said Brian.

"Not that," I said. "What's bothering me is that the auditorium door was locked. What does that tell you?"

"That it wasn't *un*locked?" said Mara.

"That this school has good security?" asked Kelly.

"That the cast didn't want us back inside the theater?" asked Brian.

"Yes, yes, and I hope not," I said. "But what the locked door *really* tells us is that the only people in the auditorium when the tuba went missing were Mrs. Rinkle and . . . the cast."

"Aha!" said Brian. "I knew it! Wait. I don't know it. What do you mean?"

Suddenly, Kelly gasped. "Jeff means . . . that someone in our show hid Violet's tuba."

Then Mara gasped. "Jeff means . . . that someone in this talent show really *does* have talent."

Finally, I gasped. "A talent . . . for crime!"

4

Crimes All Over the Place

After we told Mrs. Rinkle what we discovered, she agreed to let the Goofballs solve the mystery of the missing tuba.

In the meantime, Violet hummed the tuba parts. It went pretty well until she started drooling, and Tuesday's rehearsal ended.

Wednesday's rehearsal was cancelled because most of the cast—Brian, Mara, Kelly, Joey, Violet, and I—had a soccer game.

We lost the game, mainly because I couldn't stop thinking about Violet's tuba and accidentally let the other team score.

Ten times.

I decided that we needed my dog Sparky's help to solve the Mysterious Talent Show Mystery. Sparky is my red-and-white corgi and the official Goofdog.

"Can Sparky watch our rehearsal?" I asked Mrs. Rinkle when we arrived on Thursday.

"He'll be our audience," she said.

"Goof!" Sparky barked; then he jumped into a front-row seat and curled up.

“We have to make up for lost time,” Mrs. Rinkle said. “Who has the scripts?”

“They’re in the office,” said Billy. He hustled offstage, came back with the scripts, and passed them out.

“Everyone in position,” Mrs. Rinkle said. “Scripts open. And . . . action!”

I have to say that the play *was* pretty good. It went like this. . . .

<u>SCENE 1</u>

A jungle at dawn. The air is filled with the gentle calls of birds waking up.

On cue, Violet made loud mouth noises. *BWAAAP! BWAAAP!*

MR. PANDA *appears with a heaping plate of coconut pancakes.*

PANDA: My friend Bat should be here for breakfast. Where, oh, where is he?

GIRAFFE *and* ZEBRA *enter.*

GIRAFFE: How are you today, Panda?

PANDA: Bat is missing!

ZEBRA: Let's get River Fairy and Wood Elf. They'll help us look for him.

All exit.

<u>SCENE 2</u>

RIVER FAIRY *sings a song by a riverbank.*

Here I am by the water.

The water is blue.

I drink it sometimes.

How about you?

WOOD ELF *enters*: Knock-knock.

RIVER FAIRY: Who's there?

WOOD ELF: Me.

RIVER FAIRY: Me who?

WOOD ELF: Me, Wood Elf. You, River Fairy!

PANDA, GIRAFFE, *and* ZEBRA *enter*.

ALL THREE: Bat is mising!

All exit.

"Awesome!" Mrs. Rinkle said. "Joey, you are the official curtain raiser. Please raise the curtain!"

Joey grinned. "Yes, ma'am. I've always wanted to be an official curtain raiser!"

But when Joey tried to raise the curtain, the rope wouldn't budge. "Hey! What's wrong?"

"Maybe you're not so official," said Billy.

"You have to know the magic words," said Brian. "Open sesame seed crackers!"

Joey tugged again, but the curtain didn't go up. Then Brian and Joey tried tugging together. The curtain still didn't go up.

"Step aside, weaklings," said Mara. But when she tried pulling it, the curtain still didn't go up.

Sparky leaped onstage and grabbed the rope between his teeth. It *still* didn't go up.

Finally, we *all* hung on the curtain rope, and it *still-still-still* didn't go up!

"What *is* the problem?" asked Mrs. Rinkle.

"Maybe the rope is stuck on the catwalk," said Mara, gazing up behind the curtain.

At the word *cat*, Sparky growled and raced right up the stairs to the catwalk. There wasn't any cat for him to find, but all at once he began barking and jumping.

"Goof! Goof!"

"Sparky found a clue!" I said.

"Hold on," said Brian. He took out a very long, thin telescope made from drinking straws put together. It nearly reached the ceiling.

"The curtain rope is tied!" he said. "It's deliberately tied to the catwalk railing!"

Deliberately is a good mystery word. It means someone did something on purpose.

"Why would anyone do that?" asked Joey.

"Mystery number two," whispered Mara.

I wrote it down.

Curtain rope deliberately tied to catwalk

Mrs. Rinkle paced the stage. “I don’t understand what’s happening here, but let’s please continue reading our play.”

So we started scene three.

SCENE 3

Deeper in the jungle. Enter Panda, Giraffe, Zebra, River Fairy, and Wood Elf. They come to a big tree.

PANDA: Miss Tree, my friend Bat is missing. Can you see him from your high branches?

TREE: Yes! Bat is IN my branches!

BAT: A wild snake has trapped me here! I am too afraid to fly away.

WOOD ELF: Knock-knock.

EVERYONE ELSE: Who's there?

WOOD ELF: Wood Elf.

EVERYONE ELSE: Wood Elf who?

WOOD ELF: I *wood elf* you, but Mr. Monkey climbs trees better.

EVERYONE: Monkey! Monkey! Please come and save Bat from that wild snake!

Enter Monkey.

"And now, Billy," said Mrs. Rinkle, "it's time for Mr. Monkey's big speech. . . ."

Billy flipped to his page and said nothing.

"Speak up, Mr. Monkey," said Violet.

"I can't," said Billy.

"Why not?" asked Tiffany.

"Because all my lines are gone!"

We all looked through our scripts and found that every one of Mr. Monkey's lines was gone. As if they had never existed!

"That's mystery number three!" said Kelly.

Mrs. Rinkle frowned big-time. "This is not awesome at all. I don't know what's going on, but let's stop our rehearsal for today. Maybe tomorrow we'll have a good one."

"Of course it will be good," said Tiffany. "I'll have our costumes ready to try on."

After Mrs. Rinkle left one way and the kids left the other, I turned to my friends.

"Goofballs, front and center!" I said.

“We can all be in the front,” said Brian, “but we can’t all be in the center. I call it!”

“I do!” said Kelly.

“I do!” said Mara.

They all jumped into the same seat in the front row. They looked like a Goofball sandwich with a Goofdog on top.

"Look," I said, walking back and forth and reading my cluebook, "first, the guilty party hid Violet's tuba. I remember Tiffany saying she didn't like the sound. Maybe that's a clue. Joey seemed jealous of Billy's big part in the show, but someone tied the curtain rope, making Joey look bad. Billy is a rope expert, but then his lines were cut, so he couldn't be the culprit. We have three mysteries and no real suspect."

"Unless you count everybody," said Kelly.

"True," I said. "This is like trying to solve a big puzzle with invisible pieces."

"I like that," said Brian. "Write it down."

So I did.

Big puzzle
Invisible pieces

"We need to get to the bottom of this," I said.

"In the meantime, our guilty party is still on the loose," said Kelly.

"I hope my costume isn't loose," said Brian. "I need to look good for my family. They'll all be there to see the show."

What Brian said turned out to be a big, large, huge, and enormous clue.

But I didn't know it yet.

No one did.

5

The Big Costume Mix-up

Before school on Friday, Kelly, Brian, Mara, and I talked about the talent show mysteries.

We talked between classes.

We talked on our way to the high school.

But nothing was coming together.

"Three mysteries and no suspects," Kelly said with a sigh. "You don't have to be a math expert to know those numbers don't add up."

“*Brain* could probably add them up,” said Brian. “But he doesn’t want to right now.”

When we entered the auditorium, Mrs. Rinkle and Tiffany were carrying a big box onto the stage.

“Costumes!” Mrs. Rinkle said.

“I even made one for Sparky on my professional sewing machine,” said Tiffany.

“Goof!” said Sparky.

"That's his one line!" said Mrs. Rinkle as she set down the carton on the stage.

Suddenly, Tiffany stomped her dancing foot. "I forgot the animal hats and gloves. I'll be right back." She went up the aisle, leaving the door propped open with a shoe.

Mrs. Rinkle beamed. "We'll try these costumes on one at a time in the—"

"Me first!" cried Brian, snatching his bat suit from the carton and running into the costume room to change.

Mrs. Rinkle laughed. "That's the spirit. It shows that no matter how many delays we've had, this will be the best show—"

"Ugh! Ouch! No, you don't! Hey! HELP!"

"That's Brian in the costume room!" I said

"His hands are fighting!" said Kelly.

"Maybe it's a duel to the death!" said Mara.

But when we raced into the costume room, Brian's hands weren't swordfighting.

He was twisted up in his bat costume and desperately trying to get out.

"My arms disappeared," he cried. "And I still need them for lots of stuff!"

Brian's feet were down where the knees should be. His head was invisible. His arms were lost in big folds of fuzzy black fabric, and his bat wings flopped across the floor.

“Something about this isn’t right,” said Mrs. Rinkle.

Then Billy tried on his Mr. Monkey suit. But it came up only to his waist.

“I think this was made for my little monkey brother. And I don’t *have* a little monkey brother! Or any kind of brother!”

Kelly slipped into her River Fairy outfit. Except that it sort of slipped into her.

“What kind of River Fairy wears baggy pants?” she asked.

"River Fairies are elegant and beautiful. Like me," she said.

Mara couldn't get her actual trunk into her tree trunk. "My roots can't breathe! Help!"

None of our costumes fit.

"Let me see the measurement sheet," I said, taking it from Tiffany's costume box. It was a sheet of blue paper. "Wait a second. Weren't the measurements on a sheet of *yellow* paper? I wonder . . ." Then something occurred to me. "I have an idea. Kelly, would you try on Tiffany's zebra suit?"

"I don't look good in stripes, but okay." But when Kelly tried on Tiffany's costume, it fit her perfectly.

"I *do* look good in stripes!"

Mrs. Rinkle's jaw dropped. "What can this possibly mean?"

"It means," I said, "that someone *deliberately* switched each person's measurements to the next person on the list," I said.

"It also means that Tiffany is going to explode when she finds out," said Brian.

"Finds out what?" said Tiffany, clacking into the room with a box of animal hats and gloves. But the moment she saw the crazy zoo in front of her, she wailed loudly.

"Ohhhhh!"

She dropped the box of hats and gloves and tried on her outfit after Kelly had taken it off.

"Someone switched the measurements!" she cried. "I slaved day and night to make these costumes! All for nothing! Oh, my poor fingers worked to the bone! My fingers are my best feature. Next to my perfect cheeks, long eyelashes, and the way I tap-dance. I'll never recover by next Friday! Maybe by Saturday . . ."

"You'd better sit down," said Mrs. Rinkle.

"I can't! This costume is too tight!"

Ripppp!

Her shoulders came through the elbows.

"Tiffany's right. We should delay the show until Saturday," said Joey, trying to find where his costume ended and his legs began.

Mrs. Rinkle paced back and forth, shaking her head. "No. No. The high school needs the building on Saturday. Besides, the show must go on."

"On what?" asked Billy. "A plastic plate?"

"On a bicycle?" asked Tiffany.

"On a vacation?" asked Violet.

"On next Saturday?" asked Joey.

Mrs. Rinkle shook her head. "*On next Friday!* Children, please. Let's take the weekend to rest up. Then we'll start again bright and early Monday afternoon."

Mrs. Rinkle checked her watch. “At the end of the week, Principal Higgins will come with tickets for you for your families,” she said. “Because . . . the show must go on!”

“Goof! Goof!” said Sparky, whose tiger costume was the only one that fit.

* * *

On the following Monday, the auditorium lights wouldn’t turn on. Until Kelly found tape covering the main light switch.

On Tuesday, the bathrooms were locked, so we all had to run home early.

It rained on Wednesday, so our coach cancelled the game and we had rehearsal.

Or we *would* have had rehearsal if Mrs. Rinkle hadn't *vanished* before our eyes.

No sooner had Brian, Mara, Kelly, Tiffany, Billy, Violet, Joey, and I entered the high school than a sudden scream rang out.

"Help! Help! Oh, help!"

We raced into the auditorium.

And there was Mrs. Rinkle, slowly disappearing *into* the stage. Her big red dress billowed out around her while her whole self sank into the floor.

“Mrs. Rinkle is melting!” cried Brian. “I saw this in a movie once. She must be a witch!”

“I am not a witch!” shouted Mrs. Rinkle.

But by the time we ran up to the stage, Mrs. Rinkle and her big red hair were gone in a cloud of blue smoke!

We were completely speechless.

Except Brian.

"She said she wasn't a witch," he said. "But what do we really know about her?"

Just then, Principal Higgins came into the auditorium with a stack of tickets and a seating chart. "Hello, students. Foggy in here, isn't it?"

"Mrs. Rinkle melted away!" said Billy. "It was pretty sad. She was such a nice lady."

Principal Higgins blinked. "Whatever do you mean?"

"That she was kind and liked people," said Billy.

"Not that!" said the principal. "What do you mean she *melted away*?"

"She disappeared into the stage," said Joey. "It was awesome. Plus a little scary."

"The show can't possibly go on Friday night," said Tiffany.

"Maybe we should delay it to Saturday night," said Violet.

"Saturday?" said the principal. "Everyone knows we can't do that."

"Oh," said Violet. "I guess I forgot."

I suddenly spotted the last wisps of fog vanishing beneath the stage where Mrs. Rinkle had been. While the other kids talked among themselves, I turned to Principal Higgins and my friends.

"Sir?" I whispered. "The Goofballs can get to the bottom of these mysteries. And when I say *get to the bottom*, I mean we need to get *under* the stage, where Mrs. Rinkle went."

"Under the stage?" said Principal Higgins. "I just happen to know the way there. I was in shows here in high school, you know."

We didn't know that.

"Come along, Goofballs," he said. "And your Goofdog, too. Follow me!"

The principal zipped out the door into the hallway. And we zipped right behind him.

6

Under the Stage

We followed Principal Higgins down a short set of steps to a black door.

"We were going to go through this door when we searched for the missing tuba," said Brian.

"But Violet tried the door and said it was locked," added Mara.

Except that when we tried the door, it wasn't locked.

It swung open easily.

"That's very interesting," Principal Higgins murmured. "It's even odd."

"*Even* can't be *odd*," said Kelly. "It's mathematically impossible."

"Flashlights aren't impossible," said Mara, clicking on a mini-flashlight and pushing her big green glasses up on her nose.

"I've sharpened my swords just in case we meet any real bats," said Brian, drawing his tiny sticks out in front of him.

"Cluebook open and pencil ready," I said. "Principal Higgins, please lead the way."

"Oh, dear me," said the principal, peering into the dark area beneath the stage. "I had forgotten how gloomy this space is. It's far too creepy for someone in my position. There might be things living down there."

“Let’s hope Mrs. Rinkle is one of them,” I said.

“I’d better go and see about selling tickets,” the principal said. An instant later—*whoosh!*—he was gone.

“Now *that* was even odd,” said Mara.

“I’d have to agree,” said Kelly.

I took a deep breath and said, “All right, team, let’s . . . go!”

Together, the four of us and Sparky eased past the black door and tiptoed beneath the stage.

We ducked under the crisscrossing beams that held up the floorboards. We passed cables dangling from the ceiling. We spotted the enormous fog machine.

Sparky sniffed and snorted and sneezed the whole way.

Finally, we spied what looked like a big motor attached to a bunch of pipes attached to the floorboards above our heads.

"A trapdoor machine," said Brian. "That must be how Mrs. Rinkle vanished like a witch—"

Crunch!

"Bones!" cried Kelly. "I stepped on bones!"

Mara swung her light down. "Not quite."

There was a crumpled sheet of yellow paper under Kelly's toe. She picked it up, uncrumpled it, and gasped. "The original measurement sheet! The correct one!"

"Just like I thought," I said, looking over Kelly's shoulder, which is easy because she's so short. "Someone jumbled up the names and the measurements. . . ."

"Goof!" Sparky was standing still, pointing his nose at a stack of papers.

Brian followed Sparky's nose. He picked up the papers. "The original scripts! With Billy's lines still in them!"

"This is too, too weird," I grumbled.

"Goofball mysteries are," said Kelly.

All at once, Mara dropped her flashlight and cried out, "I'm being attacked! Help!"

"*Ve* shall come to your defense!" said Brian, jabbing into the dark with his tiny swords.

But when I scooped up the flashlight and shined it on Mara, we saw her feet tangled in Violet's big pink tuba. It was nestled in its pink blanket. Sparky was nestled in the blanket, too.

"This is clue central!" I said. I wrote it all down in my cluebook.

Trapdoor — Original scripts
Fog machine — Pink tuba
Yellow measurement sheet

"Should we bring everything upstairs so the show can go on?" Mara asked.

I wondered for a second, then shook my head. "Not yet. Let's think about this."

"Our specialty," said Kelly. "Ready . . ."

"And think!" said Mara.

Brump-bump-bump-bump!

Brump-bump-bump-bump!

While Brian supplied music, we paced, ducking so we didn't bump our heads on the beams. Sparky paced, too, but didn't have to duck. His legs are shorter than Brian's swords.

Suddenly, we heard Principal Higgins above us. "Cast, let me assure you that we're looking everywhere for Mrs. Rinkle. Meanwhile, you can buy your family tickets for the show. Goofballs, if you hear me down there, meet us at the ticket booth in the lobby!"

We heard lots of footsteps move outside the theater, to the lobby.

"Tickets?" whispered Mara. "With Mrs. Rinkle still missing? With so many mysteries still to solve?"

"And so many crimes?" said Kelly.

"And so many no suspects?" said Brian.

"How can we have five mysteries and not one guilty party?" said Kelly.

"Don't look at me," said Brian. "I may be guilty of some stuff, but I'm not a whole party. I'm only me."

Normally, Brian says goofy stuff.

But this time he said smart stuff.

In fact, he gave me an idea.

In *fact*, he gave me *the* idea!

My Goofball brain sparked and sizzled like a weekend barbecue.

"Goofballs," I said, "we need to get out to that ticket booth. We need one final clue. And we need it now!"

7

A Perfectly Goofy Disguise

We scurried up the stairs and into the lobby, where we ducked behind an empty table. No one saw us because the table was covered with a floppy tablecloth that hung all the way to the floor.

We peered over the top, and Sparky peered around the side. Principal Higgins sat in the ticket booth next to the auditorium doors.

Billy, Violet, Joey, and Tiffany stood nearby.

"We have to get over there without the rest of the cast seeing us," I whispered.

"What we need is a disguise," whispered Mara, adjusting her big green glasses.

Kelly nodded. "One of the first rules of the Goofball System for Effective Disguises is to disguise yourself as someone or something that no one looks at."

"I never look at ballet dancers," said Brian. "Should we dress up as ballet dancers? Not that I want to. I'm just saying."

"No," Mara said. "Ballerinas would attract attention. There *must* be another way. . . ."

She suddenly began to tap her chin, then—*whoosh!*—she disappeared beneath the table.

"Get under here," she whispered.

We did get under there. Sparky did, too. It was as cozy as a tent.

"What's the great disguise?" Kelly asked.

"You're under it," Mara said.

"This table?" I asked.

"This table," Mara said.

Brian frowned, then felt Mara's forehead. "No fever. And yet your idea is as nutty as a bag of trail mix."

"Please don't make me hungry," said Kelly. "I haven't eaten in an hour."

"The Goofballs have never disguised ourselves as furniture before," I said.

Mara grinned. "There's a first time for everything.

"What about eternity?" asked Brian.

Mara sighed. "There's a first time for everything *except* for eternity."

Brian nodded. "In that case, you're right!"

On her instructions, everyone except Sparky arched his or her back, and the table lifted up from the floor.

"One step," Mara whispered.

We all took one step.

"And down," Mara said.

We crouched, and the table lowered to the floor. We peeked out. No one noticed the table moving.

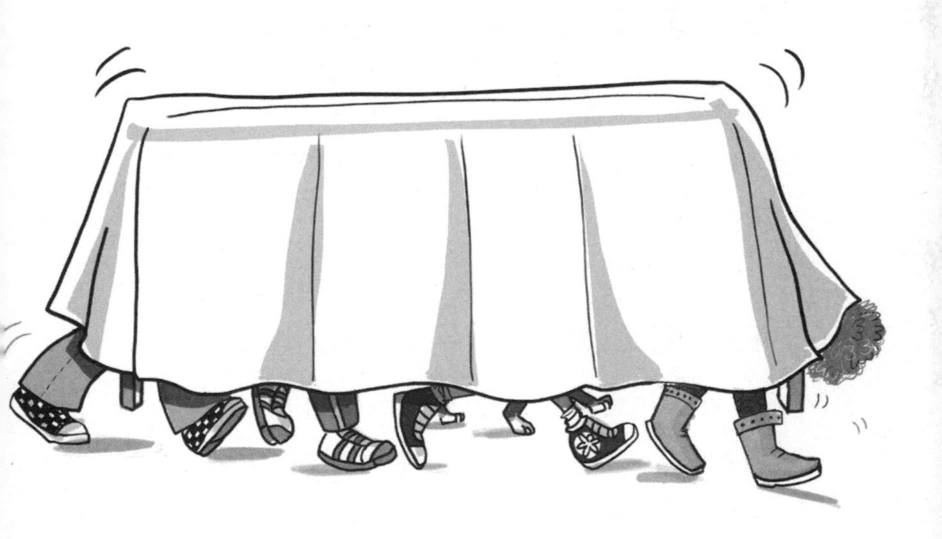

"It's working," I whispered.

We did it again. And again. And again.

Up. Step. Down. Up. Step. Down.

It probably looked pretty goofy. But most Goofball things do. The main thing was that it worked. We made our way slowly across the open space. When we finally stopped, we were a few feet away from the ticket booth.

"Good job," Kelly whispered. "The old moving-table disguise is a brand-new classic."

I peeked out and saw Principal Higgins hold up the seating chart.

"Who would like to buy tickets for Friday's show?" he asked.

That's when my brain tingled.

Because Joey, Billy, Violet, and Tiffany *all* said exactly the same thing.

"Friday night? Not Saturday night? Then, no. No, thank you."

Principal Higgins was speechless.

But I knew then what I had only suspected.

"Goofballs," I whispered. "I believe the whole big mystery really goes all the way back to the first little mystery we discovered. The sign that said 'Friturday Night.'"

"Are you saying *Friturday* was a clue?" asked Brian.

"Sort of," I said. "In fact, all the clues so far have been sort-of clues."

Kelly smiled. "Even a sort-of clue is better than no clue at all."

Which I wrote down in my cluebook, because it's so true.

Then the most amazing thing happened.

"Look at that!" I whispered.

We watched Violet, Tiffany, Billy, and Joey walk away from the ticket booth and whisper to one another. Then they all put their fingers to their lips.

"The international symbol of secrecy!" hissed Kelly. "They're all in this together!"

"Either that, or they're all chewing their nails at the same time," said Brian. "But your thing works, too."

All of a sudden, my brain sizzled like a superfast computer. It was as if the last invisible piece of the puzzle of the Talent Show Mystery snapped right into place.

"Guys," I said, "instead of looking for the person *wrecking* the show for *Friday* night, we should have been looking for the *people* who *want* the show to run on *Saturday* night!"

"And it seems like everyone does," said Mara.

"Exactly," I said. "The guilty party is exactly that. A party. Of several people."

"But why do they want the show on Saturday?" asked Brian. "And what about Mrs. Rinkle? If she's not a witch, then what happened to her?"

I thought about that. "Maybe we don't know *why* yet. Or what happened to Mrs. Rinkle. But something tells me we'll find out soon."

"Sooner than soon," said Kelly with a big Goofball grin. "There's only one place and time to catch the show wreckers."

"Where?" asked Mara.

"And when?" asked Brian.

"Onstage," Kelly said. "Friday night."

Everyone looked at me to finish it off.

So I did.

"Showtime!"

8

The Guilty Party!

As soon as the other kids left, we explained what we knew to Principal Higgins. We told him that we could show the show even if Mrs. Rinkle wasn't there. We told him that he shouldn't worry. He told us he would help us to unmask the guilty party.

Every single one of them.

"We are going to save this show," I told the Goofballs when we snuck backstage.

"But one thing I don't get," said Brian.

"Only one?" asked Mara.

"I'm in the dark about lots," said Kelly.

I gave them all a big Goofball grin. Then I told them everything I had figured out.

"Oh!" said Kelly.

"Oh!" said Mara.

"Wait. What?" said Brian.

So I told them all again. Then we crawled under the stage. We grabbed the original scripts, the yellow measurement sheet, and Violet's tuba and brought them back upstairs.

I snuck Violet's tuba back into her tuba case in the music room and snapped it closed.

Kelly and Sparky made sure that the curtain would open and close freely and that all of the scenery was in place.

Then we took the costumes and the *correct* measurements home to Mara's mom, who was great at sewing stuff.

Then Kelly and Brian wrote Billy's lines on the palms of his monkey gloves, so all he had to do was look at his hands and read them.

Mrs. Rinkle still hadn't shown up, so the rehearsal was cancelled on Thursday.

Finally, it was Friday night and time for the big show.

Principal Higgins was waiting for the cast backstage. "Children, Mrs. Rinkle has not reappeared," he said.

"So I will direct the show. I used to be in shows here, you know."

We did know.

"And now," he said, "it's showtime!"

When the curtain went up, we all bowed in front of a thousand seats filled with people.

The time to expose the whole guilty party was now or never. So I ran to center stage and shouted, "Stop the show!"

"It hasn't started yet!" someone called out.

"And it won't start," I said, "until we solve the Mysterious Talent Show Mystery!"

Mouths dropped open. People stared.

"First, let's turn back the clock nearly two weeks to our first rehearsal, last Monday afternoon," Brian said.

"To the moment Mrs. Rinkle said that the show would be performed tonight and not tomorrow night," I said. "That's when things began to happen."

"Strange things," said Mara.

"Suspicious things," said Brian.

"Criminal things!" said Kelly.

The audience gasped.

"Who did these things, you ask?" I said.

"Someone certainly was guilty," Kelly said.

"But it's not who you think," said Brian.

"It's *everyone* who you think!" Mara said as I held my cluebook high.

"This is a good show!" someone yelled out, and the audience buzzed like a beehive.

"First, Violet's tuba went missing," said Kelly.

"A dastardly crime," said Mara.

"Until you remember that Violet herself led the search for it," said Kelly. "She took us everywhere *except* under the stage, where the tuba actually was. Why? Because she *knew* it was there."

The audience gasped again.

Violet bowed her head. "I *did* hide my own tuba," she said. "I didn't want the show to go on tonight. The grand opening of Pinkworld is happening right now. I came only because my friends are in the audience. But I'm missing all that pink!"

"Except," said Mara, "the *extra-super-special* grand opening is *Sunday* evening. And, being so stylish, I have a pass you can have!"

"Really?" said Violet. "Wowee!"

"One mystery solved," said Brian. "But then came mystery two. The tying of the rope so that Joey couldn't raise the curtain. It delayed the rehearsal a second time. Who caused this delay? Joey himself!"

Joey breathed out a big sigh. "My family can't make it tonight. But they could have if the show was tomorrow. Who wants to be in a show if your family can't see you?"

We all knew what he meant. And everyone onstage except Joey took a moment to wave to our families in the audience.

"Along came mystery three," said Mara. "Billy's lines were cut from the show. Why? Let Billy himself tell you his story."

Billy walked to the center of the stage and bowed. "I took the scripts into the theater office. I cut my speech out of everybody's script. Then I put in a new page. Then I copied them for everybody. I cut my own lines because I cannot memorize lines. I can only say what I feel. And right now, I feel sorry. Thank you."

"Now mystery four!" said Kelly, who swung around to Tiffany. "You switched your own measurements, didn't you?"

Tiffany curtseyed. "I did. Because the bandage on my sprained ankle comes off tomorrow. If the show got delayed, I'd be able to dance with both feet."

That explained so much.

"That solves the missing tuba, the tied curtain rope, the switched costume measurements, and the missing lines," said Brian. "But who made Mrs. Rinkle disappear?"

"The last person in the guilty party did that," I said. "The party's hostess!"

Then I motioned to Joey, who pulled back the curtain, and there stood . . .

"Mrs. Rinkle!" everyone shouted.

Mrs. Rinkle's cheeks went redder than her red hair. "I used the fog machine and the trapdoor to make myself disappear. I thought it would delay the show, too. I didn't want the show to play just one night. I wanted more time together with these awesome kids!"

The audience applauded.

"So the crimes weren't even crimes," I said, "because the criminals did them to themselves!"

That was when Principal Higgins walked out to center stage and spoke.

"The town, the high school, and Badger Point Elementary have decided to put on the show again next weekend and the weekend after that, too!"

The whole audience stood and cheered.

Mrs. Rinkle could barely speak, she was laughing so hard. "And . . . now . . . the . . . awesome show . . . must go on!"

And it did.

The act one talent show?

Well, it went pretty much like the audition.

Except that just before I went on, Brian said, "Hey, Jeff. I have something for you." He handed me a perfect balancing stick.

"Where did you find this?" I asked.

Brian shrugged. "Backstage."

"Hey! Who stole a branch from my tree hat?" shouted Mara.

And—*whoosh!*—Brian vanished *without* a fog machine.

I finally got to balance my plate.

The audience loved it.

All three seconds.

Mr. Bat's Birthday Rescue?

It was as awesome as Mrs. Rinkle had predicted.

Everyone's costume fit perfectly. Violet's tuba birdcalls made the audience laugh. My sad search for Mr. Bat made everyone cry. Joey's Wood Elf jokes made everyone clap.

And then came Billy's part. Because his lines were written on his palms, he didn't have to remember them.

Too bad the words got smeared together when he clapped his paws so hard.

Dear Mr. Tree. Do not rescue Bat. He will climb a wild breakfast. I am afraid of coconuts. Thank you for the snakes. I hope we climb the river together. All your best friends are pancakes.

Which sounded a lot like Kelly's song.

Only it made more sense.

To end the show, Violet played a lullaby on her pink tuba that put all the dads to sleep. Until all the babies screamed. Which made the moms burst out laughing. That's when the audience cheered the loudest.

When everyone yelled for more, we did it again. Everybody loved Brain's swordfight, even if they couldn't tell which hand was winning.

When his left hand gave up, his right hand bowed to the audience.

"In stick swordfights, it's *widely* known that your right hand usually wins," Brian announced.

"Really?" I said. "It's *widely* known?"

"I know this because my name is *Brain*," he said. "But go look it up."

I would look it up, except that I haven't had time. We're still rehearsing for our next show.

And our next. And our next.

Proving that . . . the Goofballs always go on!